MILLY at Magic SCHOOL

Dedicated to Annette,
for her spiritual help and inspiraton

MYRIAD BOOKS LIMITED
35 Bishopstrophe Road, London SE26 4PA

First published in 2003 by
PICCADILLY PRESS LIMITED
5 Castle Road, London NW1 8PR
www.piccadillypress.co.uk

Text and illustration copyright © Jane Andrews, 2003

The right of Jane Andrews to be recognised as Author of this work has been asserted by her
in accordance with the Copyright, Designs and Patants Act 1988.

ISBN: 1 904736 64 5

Designed by Louise Millar

Printed in China

Milly at Magic School

Jane Andrews

MYRIAD BOOKS LIMITED

Today was Milly's first day at Magic School and she was really
excited. She had worked very hard to pass the entrance exam –
Magic School wasn't easy to get into!

Mrs Marsh, the Head Mistress, was waiting at the front door
to greet the children.

Ms Divine, Milly's new teacher, introduced her to the class and said that Milly was a 'star pupil'.

Most of the children staring back at Milly were smiling, except for three girls in the front row, Prunella, Beatie and Floe.

They started to pull faces. Why should *they* want a 'star pupil' in *their* class?

When the lessons began, strange things started to happen to Milly. First, her pen wouldn't write. Nothing appeared on the paper! She tried three different pens and a pencil, but none of them worked. Ms Divine noticed. "This is odd, Milly. Why don't you try the blackboard instead?"

But the chalk went completely out of control when Milly picked it up.
"Dear me, this sort of behaviour won't do," said Ms Divine,
thinking it was all Milly's fault.
Milly saw Prunella, Beatie and Floe laughing at her. She felt
embarrassed and cross.

The next day was even worse. Just before lunch, Milly's hair suddenly stood straight up in the air. And it started to grow upwards right in front of everyone's eyes!

And then her tunic turned bright pink.

"Something is very wrong here," said Ms Divine to Milly.

"I think you'd better see the school nurse at once."

Milly sat down in the nurse's chair feeling very low.

"Hmm, I think someone has been playing magic tricks on you," said the nurse.

Milly was too shocked to say anything, but then she thought of Prunella, Beatie and Floe.

"Your tunic will go back to blue soon, but I'll just go and get
something special for your hair," said the nurse, very kindly.
While she was gone, Milly looked around the room. It was
full of jars, bottles and books. She saw that one large book
was lying open.

Milly carefully turned the pages of the book. It was full of magic potions! She suddenly remembered Prunella, Beatie and Floe laughing at her.

"This could come in handy," she thought.

She found one called "Wild Shoes" and memorised it. Then she quickly shut the book as the nurse returned.

Milly had to drink a terrible-tasting potion, but, thank goodness, her hair turned back to normal!

Back home, Milly thought and thought about the spell. Where could she get hair of hog? When she patted her dog Dido she suddenly knew what to do.

She mixed up the potion using dog's hair, not hog's hair, and fish food instead of old fish bones.

Milly decided to try the spell out on her fish, Sven, just to be
safe. She put a pinch of the potion in the goldfish bowl.
"*Make this fish have a mind of its own!*"
Poor Sven! He jumped out of his bowl, wiggled up the wall and
somersaulted, and then plopped back down into his bowl.
"Wow!" said Milly.

Next day when everyone was ready for gym, Milly carefully sprinkled some of her potion into Prunella, Beatie and Floe's gym shoes. They were too busy talking to notice anything.
"Hair of hog and old fish bones,
Make these shoes have a mind of their own,"
whispered Milly.

Everyone was working hard at their stations, when suddenly there was a lot of noise.
Prunella, Beatie and Floe stumbled across the gym floor.
"Help!" screeched the three girls as they spun, whirled and rolled around.

FIZZ!

BANG!

POP!

went their gym shoes.

Eventually the shoes ran out of steam and the three girls crumpled in a heap on the ground. Everyone else was laughing, and Milly had a big smile on her face.

"I think someone has played a clever trick," said the gym teacher, Mr Lean, looking sideways at Milly. "I'll have to have a stern talk with whoever did this."

The surprising thing was that once Prunella, Beatie and Floe had recovered they couldn't stop talking about what had happened.

They bombarded Milly with all sorts of questions about how she had made the magic potion and how it worked.

They even invited her to sit with them at lunch. Milly was happy
to be their friend, but she didn't want there to be any more
nasty tricks.
So all four girls agreed only to use magic to be helpful and not
for mischief.

And Milly never ever told anyone about the 'Wild Shoes' spell and where she had found it!